Mysterious Tales of
Arabian Nights

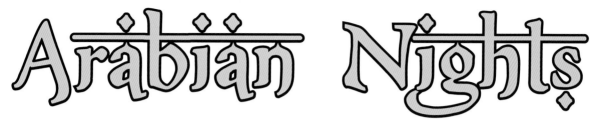

An imprint of Om Books International

Reprinted 2014

Published by

An imprint of Om Books International

Corporate & Editorial Office
A 12, Sector 64, Noida 201 301
Uttar Pradesh, India
Phone: +91 120 477 4100
Email: editorial@ombooks.com
Website: www.ombooksinternational.com

Sales Office
4379/4B, Prakash House, Ansari Road
Darya Ganj, New Delhi 110 002, India
Phone: +91 11 2326 3363, 2326 5303
Fax: +91 11 2327 8091
Email: sales@ombooks.com

ISBN : 978-81-87107-94-1

Printed in India

10 9 8 7 6 5 4

Contents

The Merchant and the Genie

Once upon a time, there lived a rich merchant. One day, he had to travel to another city for business. On his way, he had to pass through a desert.

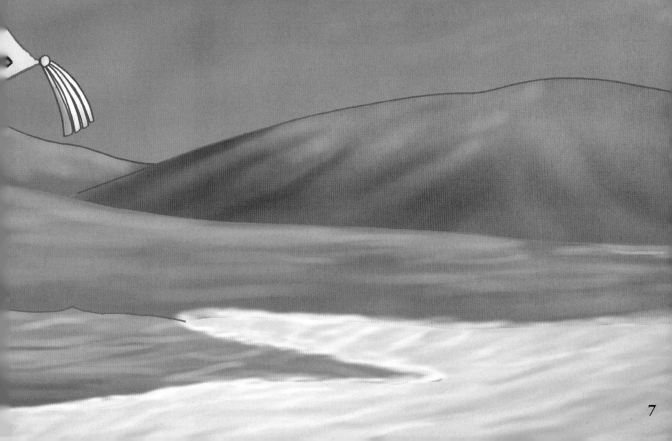

So he carried with him a small packet of dates and biscuits to eat on the way.

On the fourth day of his journey, he saw clear water. He ran towards it and after having water to drink and washing his face, he gave his tired horse some water to drink.

While he was giving the horse water, suddenly he heard a loud noise. It looked as if a storm was approaching. When he looked closely, he saw a genie with a huge sword in his hand running towards him.

The genie caught him by the arm and said, "I will kill you the way you killed my son." The merchant was shocked. He said, "I think you have made some mistake. I did not kill anyone. I am just a simple merchant on my way to another city." But the genie replied, "You are a murderer. You just killed my son."

The merchant kept telling the genie that he had not killed anyone. So the genie told him, "Did you not sit on the ground just before having water?" The merchant nodded.

11

"Did you not eat some dates and throw the seeds around?" asked the genie. The merchant nodded at this too. "So, at that time, my son was passing by and one of the seeds hit him in the eye and killed him." The merchant had nothing to say. He had not seen or heard anything like this before.

"Oh great genie! I beg you to pardon me. After all, I did not kill your son with any intention to do so," cried the merchant. But the genie was adamant. He said, "I will have to kill you. So prepare to die."

Then the merchant said, "At least, give me some time to bid farewell to my family and then kill me." The genie said, "If I allow you to leave, you will never come back."

But the merchant promised to return. So the genie asked him, "How much time do you need to come back?" "Just one year," replied the merchant.

So the genie let him go and the merchant
returned home — a sad man! He told everyone
in his family about the genie and that he had
just one year to get back.

The very next day, he started paying off all his debts. He set all his slaves free. He worked all through the year making money for his family and gave lots of presents to his friends

and family. Finally, a year had passed by and the merchant set out for the place where he had met the genie for the first time.

While he waited for the genie, he saw an old man with a red deer walking towards him. The old man said, "Brother, why are

you sitting at this place where a lot of evil genii are around?" The merchant told him his sad story.

To that, the old man replied, "I have never seen anything like this before. So I will wait with you to see what happens." So saying, he sat down next to the merchant. After some time, another old man came by with two black dogs. He too asked the merchant the same

question, which the first man had asked and decided like him to sit with the merchant. Soon, another old man also came by and sat with the merchant like the others.

"Look!" said the men, "There is a cloud of smoke coming towards us." "That is the genie," said the merchant.

"Are you ready to die?" asked the genie.
Hearing this, the first old man fell at the feet of
the genie and said, "Oh Prince of the Genii, please
listen to the story of this red deer here, and me.

And, if you find that better than the merchant's story, please pardon him one-third of his life." The genie thought for a while and agreed.

And so began the first old man's story...

The First Old Man

The first old man began his story to the genie. He said, "This red deer that you see is my wife."

"Once upon a time, I lived in a small town with my wife. But I had no son," said the old man. He continued with his story saying,

"I adopted the son of my favourite servant. But my wife did not like the servant or the son."

She told me, "How can you make the son of a servant your heir?" "But I was adamant as I loved the boy."

"One day, I had to leave for a journey. I left the son and the servant in my wife's care," said the old man to the genie. "But my evil wife learnt magic from someone and turned the servant into a cow and my son into a calf."

"When I returned after a few months and asked for my son, she told me that my servant was dead and my son had gone missing. After a month or so, there was a feast in the house. I asked my servant to bring a cow to sacrifice."

"When the servant brought a cow — which was actually my servant before my wife's magic — it came running to me and cried seeing me." "I was moved by the tears of the cow and asked my servant to take it away."

"When my wife saw this, she came running to me and asked me to sacrifice it. I was not too happy to do it, but my wife forced me to do so." "Finally, the cow was killed and all that was there of it was bones, though it looked fat from the outside."

"After that, I asked for a fat calf." "The servant brought a calf, which leapt with joy on seeing me. I was so moved to see it so happy, that I asked it to be taken away." "My wife begged me to kill it, but I did not."

"The next day, my servant came to see me and said he had some news for me." He said, "My daughter knows magic and said, the calf that you saw yesterday was actually your son

and the cow, which we killed was your servant." "I was very very sad to hear the news. I rushed to the shed to meet my son, the calf, with the servant's daughter."

"I asked her to turn the calf back into my son." She said, "I will, if you promise to marry him to me and allow me to turn your evil wife into a red deer." "I agreed, and that's how you see my wife as this red deer."

The genie was very happy
to hear the story. He said, "Your story really
moved me." Just then the second old man
said, "Now hear my story and grant this
merchant another one-third of his life."

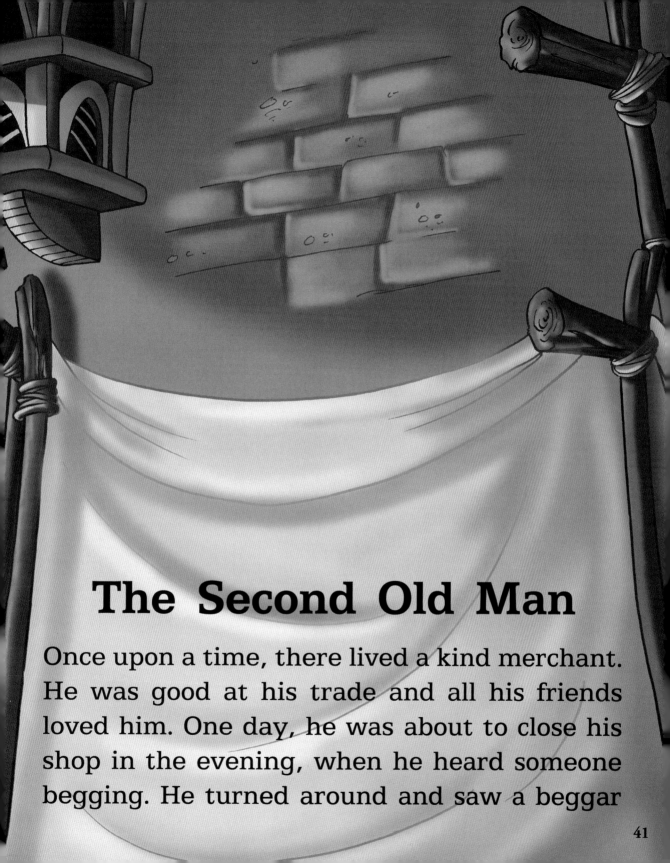

The Second Old Man

Once upon a time, there lived a kind merchant. He was good at his trade and all his friends loved him. One day, he was about to close his shop in the evening, when he heard someone begging. He turned around and saw a beggar in rags. He looked very sick, but somewhere he also looked familiar. The merchant thought to himself, "Where have I seen him?"

In a flash, he recognized that it was his brother. When his father died, he had left his three sons, a thousand coins each. The three brothers had each started a shop. However, his elder brother wanted to travel and set out with a caravan. After that no one had heard of him, till the merchant saw him as a beggar in front of his shop.

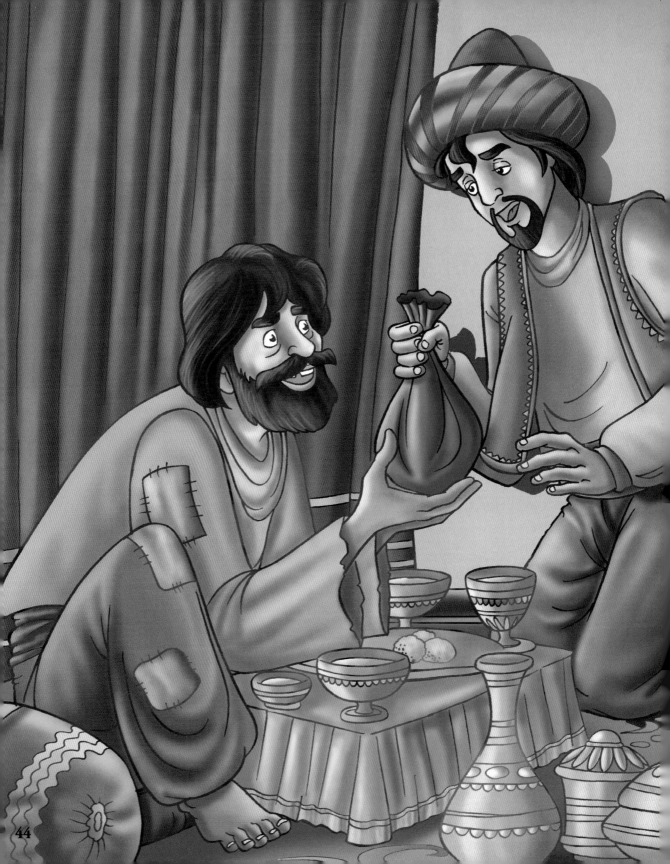

The merchant was indeed shocked and asked his brother, "Where have you been and what happened to all your money?" The brother replied, "I lost all my money while traveling. I have nothing now." The merchant took pity on his brother and took him home. He gave him a thousand more coins and asked him restart his shop.

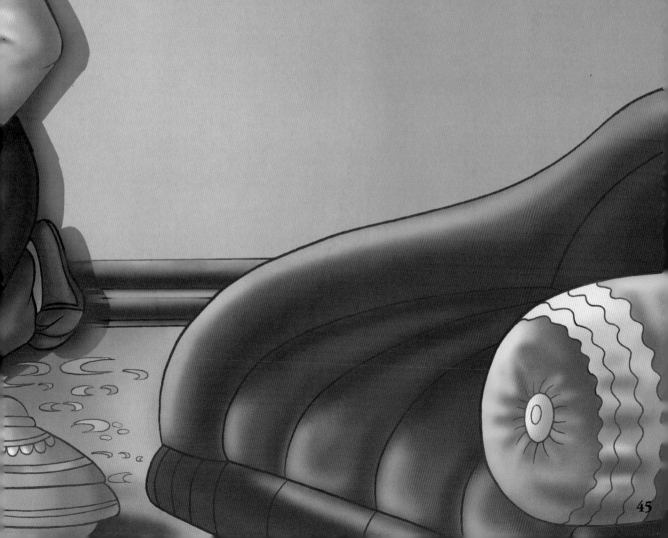

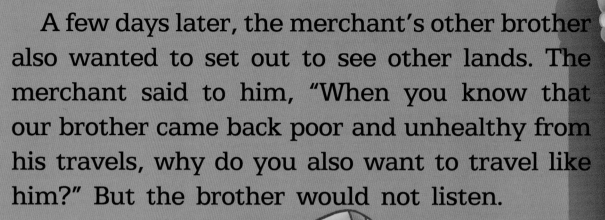

A few days later, the merchant's other brother also wanted to set out to see other lands. The merchant said to him, "When you know that our brother came back poor and unhealthy from his travels, why do you also want to travel like him?" But the brother would not listen.

He set out and returned a year later, just like the elder brother — having lost all his money! The merchant took pity on him and gave him a thousand coins too.

However, after a few years, the brothers started to pester the merchant about their desire to travel again. The merchant refused them for five years. But one fine day, accepted. When they began their preparations for the journey, the merchant gave his brothers a thousand coins each and kept a thousand for himself. He buried three thousand coins in a corner of his house. And finally, all the three brothers set out sailing.

They reached port after a few months of sailing. The port was full of lovely things. The merchant and his brothers happily bought a lot of things and were about to sail back, when

a woman in rags came up to the merchant. She held his hand, kissed it and said, "Will you marry me?" The merchant was surprised, but the woman insisted.

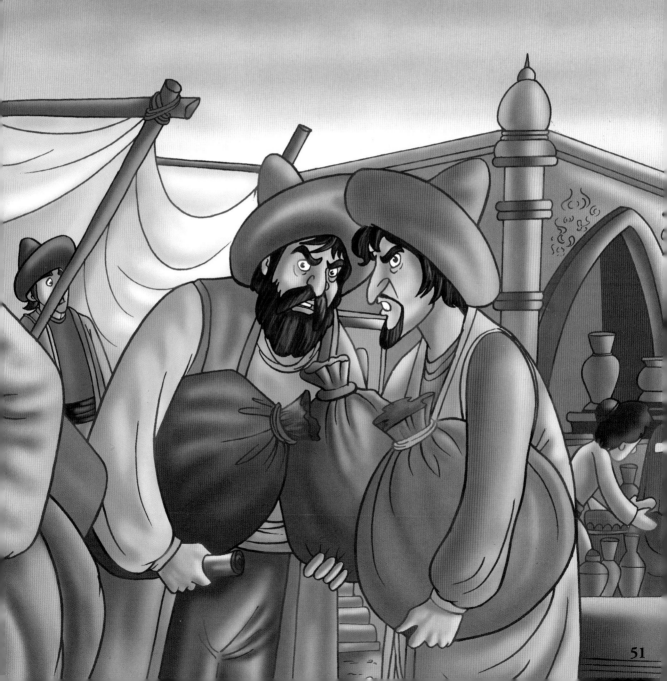

The merchant finally agreed and took her on board. After they set sail, he gave her lovely clothes to wear and good food to eat. The woman became more beautiful by the day. The merchant also loved her more and more with each passing day.

But the merchant's evil brothers plotted against him. One night, they threw the merchant and his wife off the ship. But the woman was in reality a fairy. So, she did not drown and saved her husband, the merchant, from drowning. She transported him magically to an island. There she told him the true story of his brothers.

The merchant said, "My lovely wife, forgive their sins. They will be punished for their acts." The fairy accepted the merchant's pleas and with a swish of her wand transported him to his house.

The merchant was delighted to get back to his house and meet his friends. He dug up the coins he had buried in his house and

returned to his shop. After a few days, he saw two black dogs in front of his shop. As he was about to drive them away, the fairy reappeared and said, "Your brothers have reaped the fruit of their sins. I changed them

into dogs for ten years, as a punishment for
their act."

The merchant took his brothers, in the form
of dogs, home and looked after them, waiting
for the spell to be broken!

The third old man also narrated his story to the genie. The genie was pleased and gave the merchant the last one-third of his life. "Thank your friends for narrating their lovely stories and buying freedom for you," said the genie and went his way.

The merchant thanked all the three old men for getting him back his life. "I will always remain thankful to you. If there is anything I can do for anyone of you to break your spells, count on me!" said the merchant and ran home to his family — a free and happy man!

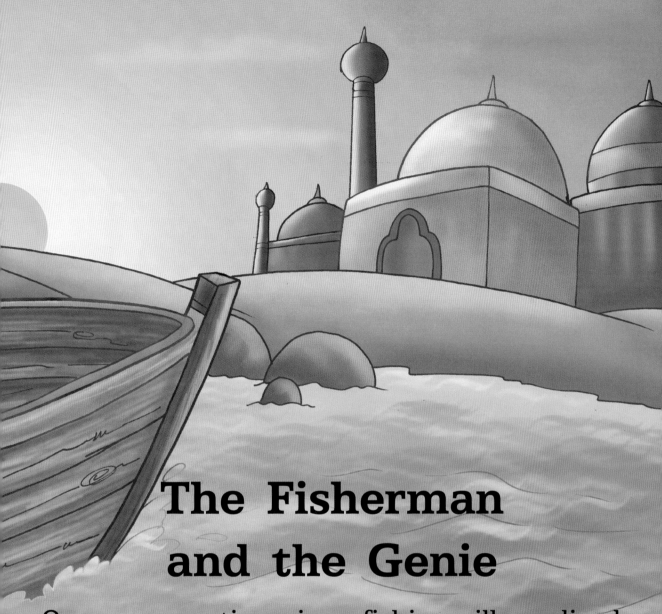

The Fisherman
and the Genie

Once upon a time, in a fishing village, lived a poor fisherman. He was the most hard-working fisherman in the village, as he would go to work before everybody and return after they all returned.

But his wife always complained and said, "You are good for nothing! You never get fish the way the others do."

One day, the fisherman reached the banks really early in the morning. He threw his net and found that it felt very heavy. He thought,

"I am finally lucky! It must be a big catch in there." He pulled the net with a lot of excitement. But alas! it was just the skeleton of a donkey.

The disappointed fisherman again cast the net and this time too, the net felt heavy. But like the earlier time, it came back with a lot of rubbish. The fisherman was determined

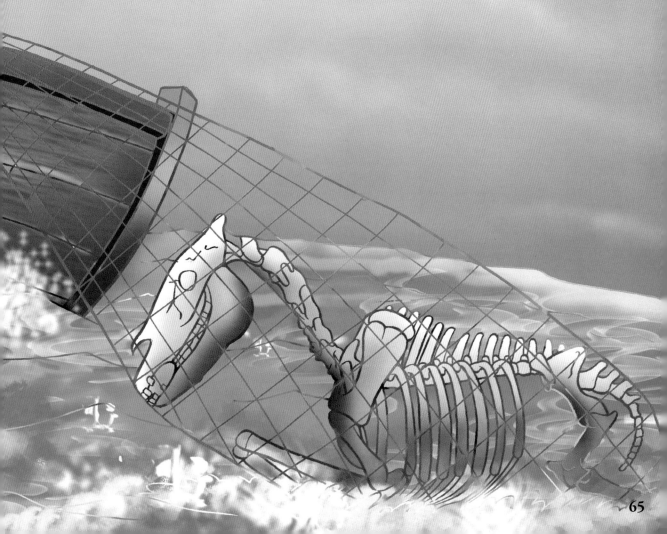

and cast his net a third time. This time, he pulled back a pot, which was sealed from all sides. There was something written on the pot, but the fisherman could not understand it. He thought to himself, "I will sell this in the market for a good price." But then he thought, what would he say it contained?! He shook it to guess what it was. But, he could not feel anything. So he decided to open it and check.

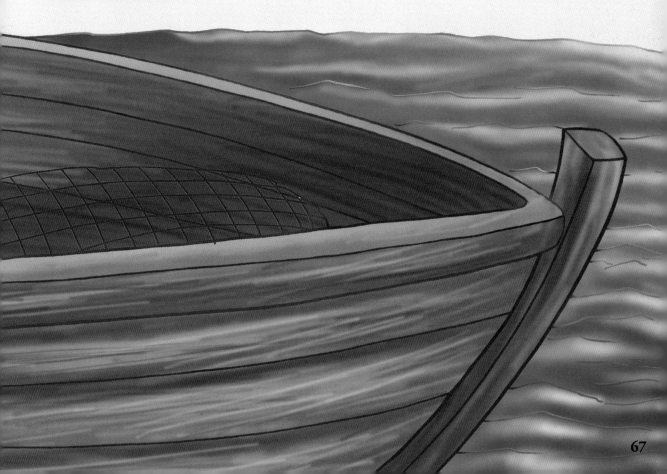

The moment he opened the seal and the lid with his knife, a huge cloud of black smoke arose into the sky. The cloud took the form of a genie.

"So how would you like to die?" roared the genie. "How unfaithful can you get?" asked the fisherman. "I just set you free and you want to kill me?" shouted the fisherman.

"It is destiny," said the genie. "I fought with the King of the Genii and he punished me by locking me inside this pot and throwing it inside the sea." "I have been inside the sea for four centuries. In the first century, I vowed that if someone set me free, I would make him rich even after his death. But no one

came! In the second century, I vowed that I would make the person who releases me the richest man in the world. Yet, I was not set free. In the third century, I vowed that I would make the man who releases me King of the

land and grant him three wishes every day. But no one set me free. Finally, after a lot of sadness, I vowed that I would kill the man who set me free, but would allow him to choose the way he would like to die. And, you set me free!" said the genie.

"So, I do not want to kill you. But I cannot break my vow. Let me know how you would like to die," said the genie. The fisherman begged him to re-think his vow, but the genie would not listen.

The fisherman did some quick thinking and said, "I cannot still believe one thing." "And, what is that?" asked the genie.

"How could someone as huge as you, get into that small pot? You are lying to me about your story," said the fisherman.

"I am not lying," said the genie angrily. "Let me show you how I can get into that!" he said and slowly the huge genie started getting back to the black cloud he was. A little later,

that black cloud became thinner and thinner and got into the pot. "Can you now see that I am not lying?" asked the genie from inside the pot. But the clever fisherman did not

waste even a second. He closed the lid of the
pot and sealed it instantly. The genie realized
what the clever fisherman had done and said,
"Free me and I will make you rich!"

But the fisherman replied, "I will not! I can be a fool once, but not a second time." He then threw the pot back into the sea and went home a happy man!

TITLES IN THIS SERIES

  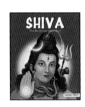 

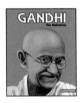

Treasure Trove of

Arabian Nights

An imprint of Om Books International

Reprinted 2014

Published by

An imprint of Om Books International

Corporate & Editorial Office
A 12, Sector 64, Noida 201 301
Uttar Pradesh, India
Phone: +91 120 477 4100
Email: editorial@ombooks.com
Website: www.ombooksinternational.com

Sales Office
4379/4B, Prakash House, Ansari Road
Darya Ganj, New Delhi 110 002, India
Phone: +91 11 2326 3363, 2326 5303
Fax: +91 11 2327 8091
Email: sales@ombooks.com

ISBN : 978-81-87107-96-5

Printed in India

10 9 8 7 6 5 4

Contents

Alibaba and the Forty Thieves

Long ago, in a small town in Persia, lived two brothers — Kasim and Alibaba. Their father had died and the two brothers had divided the wealth equally among themselves. But both spent the money quite quickly. Kasim married the daughter of a rich merchant and became the owner of a big shop with expensive things. However, Alibaba got married to a poor and needy woman. He lived on the dry wood he

collected from the jungle and sold at the market in the town.

One day, when Alibaba had cut the wood and loaded his donkeys, he saw a huge dust storm at a distance. When he looked closely,

he saw that it was actually men on horses coming towards him. "Oh! They seem to be thieves coming this way! They will kill me if I stay here. I must run and hide myself!" panicked Alibaba. He climbed and hid himself

on top of a tree and had tied his donkeys behind a bush. Alibaba had been right; these men were thieves! They rode till they reached a cave. Alibaba could see the cave in front of him, sitting on top of the tree.

The thieves were forty in all. Their leader stood in front of the cave and said, "Open Sesame!" Alibaba was stunned to see that the cave opened in front of his eyes and all the thieves went inside. When the last of the

thieves had entered, the leader again
said, "Shut Sesame!" and the cave closed.
   After a few hours, the cave opened and the
thieves rode out on their horses. After they
had traveled a safe distance, Alibaba came

down from the tree and thought to himself, "Why don't I also try the magical words and see if the cave opens?" So he stood in front of the cave and said with all confidence, "Open Sesame!" There was a loud rumbling and the cave opened. Alibaba entered the cave and what did he see? Diamonds, gold and precious jewels everywhere! "This must be the place where the thieves have been hiding their stolen treasures for years. I must carry some home," thought Alibaba. He filled his sacks

with gold and jewels and walked out of the cave, saying the magical words and shutting it behind him.

When Alibaba reached home with the gold, his wife thought he had become a robber. She

screamed at him, "Ali! I thought you were an honourable man! How could you turn into a thief? Where did all this wealth come from?" But Alibaba surprised her with his story. Alibaba's wife was now overjoyed to know

that they had indeed become rich. So she ran to Kasim's house to borrow a balance. Kasim's wife was a smart lady. She was curious to know what it was that poor Alibaba's wife

wanted to weigh. So she put some wax under the balance and gave it to Alibaba's wife. "Here you go sister! Keep it for as long as you want." Alibaba and his wife weighed the gold and put it away in a little hole that they dug up in their house. But one little coin had got

stuck to the wax. When the balance was returned to Kasim's wife, she took one look and shouted at her husband, "Do you know that your brother has been making money while you have been lazing around? Find out what he has been doing right away!"

Kasim spoke to Alibaba the next morning and learnt how he had been plain lucky. "It's all about those magical words — "Open Sesame"

and "Shut Sesame". But I urge you not to take the risk my brother. The thieves might find out," said Alibaba. But Kasim would not listen and rode to the cave. "Open, Sesame!" shouted Kasim and the cave opened. Seeing all the

treasures, Kasim was overjoyed. He filled his sacks with the treasures and finally came to the opening. But in all his excitement, he had forgotten the magic words! He said every word other than "Sesame." "Open Barley,

Open Summey, Open Stoney ..." But nothing worked. By this time, the thieves were on their way to the cave. They threw the cave open with "Open Sesame" and found poor Kasim shivering with fear. They killed him instantly and hung his dead body inside the cave as a message for other trespassers.

When Kasim did not return, his worried wife ran to Alibaba's house. "Brother, Kasim has not returned and I hope he is not in some danger. Will you please look for him?" said

23

Kasim's wife to Alibaba. Alibaba rode to the cave the next morning and found his brother's body inside the cave. "Oh my dear brother! I had warned you!" cried Alibaba. Then, hurriedly

24

he put his brother's body on his mules and rode back home.

Kasim's wife wept and wept on seeing her dead husband. He had paid for his greed with his life!

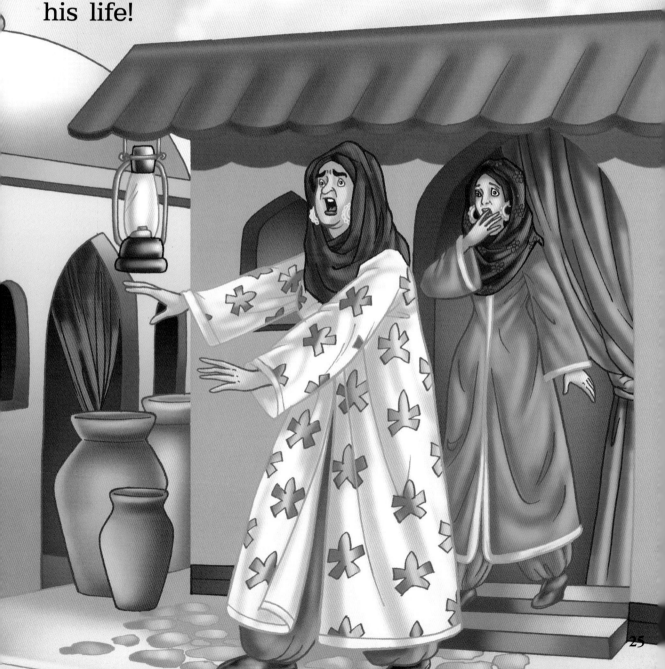

Kasim had an intelligent and beautiful slave called Marjenah, who had served him loyally.

When Kasim died, she helped Alibaba in burying him taking care that no one in the village found out.

But, at the cave, the forty thieves who found the dead body missing were planning on finding out who had come to know about their secret cave. "It is surely someone from the nearby village," said a thief to the Chief.

"So, go to the village and find out who knows our secret!" thundered the Chief.

The thief found the house from the tailor who had helped Marjenah to sew Kasim's dead body. Alibaba now lived in it! "I will put a cross mark and come back with the rest of my friends tonight," thought the robber and ran back to bring the other thieves.

That night, all the robbers came back to the village. Alas! There were cross marks on all houses. Clever Marjenah had seen one of the robbers putting the mark and knew that the thieves had found out about Alibaba. So, she put the same cross mark outside every house.

After many such attempts to find and kill Alibaba, the Chief himself came to the village and found the house. He then made a plan with the thieves. "You will all get inside these 39 jars with your weapons. One jar for each

of you! I will take this jar filled with oil and load all of you on to these mules. I will dress up as an oil merchant and visit Alibaba as a guest. I will signal all of you by throwing some stones out of the window. When you hear the

sound of the stones, rush out of your jars and attack him!" said the Chief.

As planned, the oil merchant visited Alibaba's house and asked him to give him a place for the night to rest his mules and also keep his

jars. Alibaba agreed to this. "Get my bath ready, and also prepare some good food for me and our guest," said Alibaba to Marjenah. "Alas! There is no oil in the house! Let me take some oil from the merchant's jars quickly,"

thought Marjenah. When she went and opened one of the jars, the thief inside the other thought it was time to jump out. So he asked in a soft tone, "Is it time yet, Master?" thinking it was the Chief outside.

Marjenah thought quickly. She replied in a hoarse voice like a man, "Not yet!" Marjenah touched all the jars softly and every thief asked her the same question and she gave the same answer — "Not yet!"

Then she quietly took the entire oil from the first jar and heated it. She poured some of the oil in each jar — killing all the thieves one by one. When the Chief threw out some stones to signal to his crew, he was surprised to see that

not one of his friends came out of the jars. When he quietly slipped out and looked inside the jars, he was shocked. "They are dead! Each one of them! Someone killed all my friends and I did

not even know about it!" thought the Chief. He took his horse and rode away to the forest.

Not finding his guest at the dinner table, Alibaba shouted at Marjenah. But when she showed Alibaba the dead thieves in the jars, he was surprised.

The Chief could not rest in his cave with all his friends dead. So, he came back to the village after a few years as a silk merchant

and was invited by Alibaba for dinner. Marjenah performed her best dance ever, and at the end saved her master by pulling out the dagger hidden under the silk garment of the merchant.

Alibaba let the Chief ride away into the forests, never to return! He married his only son to Marjenah. Alibaba visited the cave after a year and found all the gold where it was!

After a few years, he shared the secret of the cave with his son, and everyone lived happily ever after.

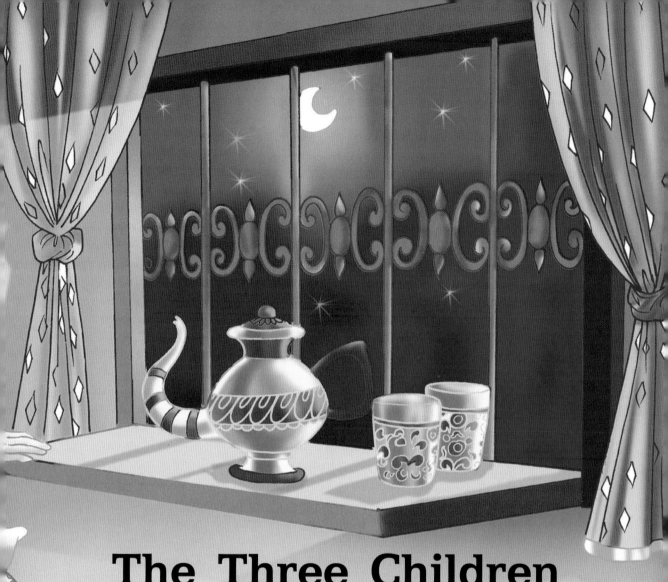

The Three Children

Once upon a time, in a little village lived three sisters. The two elder sisters were quite mean to their youngest sister. One night, they were sitting near the window and telling each other about their wishes. The eldest sister said, "How I wish I could marry the King's baker! Imagine all the delicious bread and pastries I could eat!" The middle sister said, "How I wish I could marry the King's cook! Imagine all the royal food I could get to eat!" The youngest sister said, "How I wish I could marry the

King himself!" Everyone laughed and went to sleep. No one knew that the King was doing his rounds of the kingdom dressed as a poor man and had heard everything.

So the next day, the King called all the three sisters to his court and said very kindly,

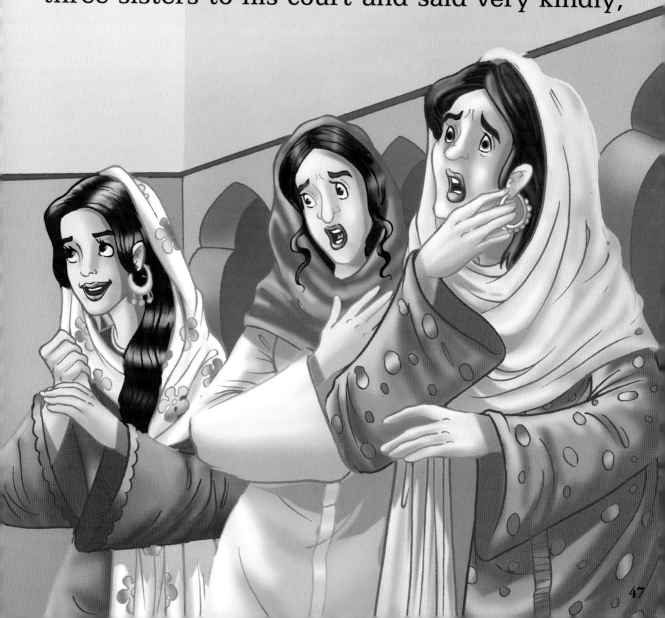

"All your wishes will be fulfilled! You—the eldest will marry my baker; you—the middle one, will marry my cook and finally, you—my pretty lady, will marry me!"

The weddings took place with great pomp. But the two elder sisters were very jealous of their youngest sister, who was now the queen. One day, there was news that the queen was going to have a baby. The two sisters planned that they would trick the King. So when the queen delivered a boy, the two sisters stole him out of the palace and put him in a basket. Then they let the basket flow away in the water of a stream.

They placed a puppy in the queen's cradle at the palace. The King was shocked to see the puppy. He said, "How can a lady give birth to a puppy?" Everyone started doubting the queen. Many called her a witch. This happened the next two times also, when the queen gave birth to two more babies—another boy and a girl. The sisters put another puppy and kitten in place of the babies and let the babies flow away in their baskets in the same stream. The

King was very angry at this strange situation. He ordered the queen to be taken away and put in prison.

But, far away where the stream ended, lived the King's guard. He did not have any

children. So, all these years, he had lifted all the babies out of their baskets and raised them as his own. He had a very big house with a lovely garden, where the children played and grew up happily!

When the eldest boy was sixteen years of age, the guard passed away. The brothers looked after their sister—Parizade—very fondly. One day, when the brothers were out hunting, an old lady visited their house. She told Parizade, "You have a beautiful garden, but there are magical things, which are far better than this." The young girl asked her what they were. The old woman replied, "The Talking Bird, whose voice draws all the birds to join it; the Singing Tree, where every leaf is a song that is never silent; and the Golden Water, of

which one drop is enough to make a fountain shoot out of it. And that fountain never stops." Parizade was fascinated by all the three. When her brothers returned, she told them about it. The eldest brother set out on his horse to get his sister the three things. He gave her a sword before leaving and said, "Keep this with you carefully. The day you see blood on it, you will know that I have died. But do not worry, nothing will happen!"

The brother set out on the path the old woman had told Parizade. After days of riding, he saw a saint on the road. He asked him where these three things could be found. The saint said, "I will give you a ball of wool, which will roll in front of you. Get down where it

stops. There will be a mountain of rocks in front of you with lots of stone people. All those people were also like you—they went to find these three magical things and became stone. You have to be careful that till you reach the Talking Bird's cage, you should not look behind

you—whatever you hear. Otherwise you will be turned into stone." The brother took the ball of wool and rode till the mountain. But when he was climbing the mountain he could not take the angry words that he heard and turned back. Alas! He had turned into stone.

Back home, Parizade suddenly saw a drop of blood on the sword. She wept at her brother's loss. The second brother set out the next day, saying that he would rescue his elder brother and bring back the other things. He too met the saint and went up the mountain,

but unfortunately, turned into stone when he looked back.

Finally, it was Parizade's turn. She rode bravely on the path her brothers had. She met the saint and took the ball of wool. Before she reached the mountain, she stuffed her ears with cotton. So when she climbed up the mountain, the voices were not so disturbing. She got to the Talking Bird's cage and brought it down with her. The bird guided her to the other two—the Singing Tree, of which she took just a twig to plant in her garden; and the

Golden Water. Then the bird told her to pick up the pitcher of water lying at the edge of the mountain and sprinkle it on all the statues of stone. As soon as Parizade sprinkled the water, all the statues came to life. Her brothers hugged her dearly and returned home.

People heard of the magical things in Parizade's house and came from far away lands to see them. One day, the King was hunting in the forest near their home. The brothers saw him, and invited him for lunch. Parizade did not know what to cook and asked the

Talking Bird, who told her to make cucumber stuffed with pearls. Parizade thought that the bird had lost his mind! But the bird insisted. The King arrived for lunch and before sitting for his meal saw the three magical things in the house. When he sat down to eat his lunch,

his teeth were hurt by the pearls. He said, "The cucumber is very well-cooked, but I do not understand the reason for the pearls." To this, the Talking Bird replied from his cage, "Surely, understanding pearls inside the cucumber would be easier than understanding that a

woman can have pups and kittens as children!"
The King was shocked to hear this. The bird
told him about how evil the sisters had been
and how kind his queen was. He also told him
that the boys and girl he saw before him were
his children.

The King apologized to the children for his folly and went back to the Kingdom with them. He united them with their mother. And all the three magical things had a special place in the palace of the King ever after...

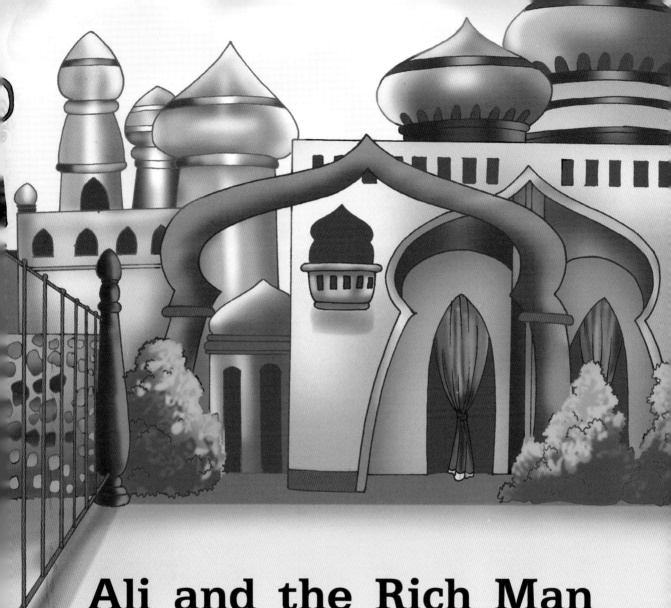

Ali and the Rich Man

Ali was very poor. Every morning, he would set out with his begging bowl. One day, he stopped in front of a mansion. He asked the guard for alms. But the guard asked him to go inside and ask the servants. The servants in turn, guided him to their master—an old man wearing rich clothes and a lot of jewellery.

The rich man said, "Sit here," and showed a chair in front of him to Ali. "Bring us some food," said the man. Then he washed his

hands with water. But Ali was puzzled! There was no water.

The rich man was acting as if someone was pouring water and that he was washing his hands. "Wash your hands," said the man to

Ali, who also acted like the man. "Put the dishes here," said the man. Again, Ali saw that there was no one and there were no dishes! "Have the meat!" said the man. Ali

acted as if he was biting into it. "Don't you want some bread?" asked the man. Ali nodded and the man acted as if he was passing a basket full of bread.

Finally, it was time for dessert. The man called for it and as usual, Ali and he acted as if their stomachs were full and they hardly had place to eat the dessert.

Ali rose from his chair, having acted enough about the meal. But the rich man laughed loudly and said, "Sit down my man!"

"I was just testing you! I wanted to see how much patience you have in following orders," said the man. "You followed my actions, and trusted me, even without knowing what I was doing. These are the qualities of a bright man. I am always in need of men like you. Stay with me," said the man. And, Ali who had gone for begging to his house for a day stayed in his house all his life.

TITLES IN THIS SERIES

  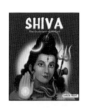 

   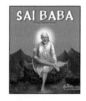

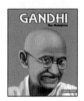